Katie Morag
and the Two Grandmothers

To all Grandmothers - Big or Wee

KATIE MORAG AND THE TWO GRANDMOTHERS
A RED FOX BOOK 978 1 782 95365 4

First published in Great Britain by The Bodley Head,
an imprint of Random House Children's Publishers UK
A Random House Group Company

The Bodley Head edition published 1985
Red Fox edition published 1997
Red Fox edition re-issued 2010
This Red Fox colour reader edition published 2014

3 5 7 9 10 8 6 4 2

Copyright © Mairi Hedderwick, 1985

The right of Mairi Hedderwick to be identified as the author of this work has been
asserted in accordance with the Copyright, Designs and Patents Act 1988.

All rights reserved. No part of this publication may be reproduced, stored in a
retrieval system, or transmitted in any form or by any means, electronic, mechanical,
photocopying, recording or otherwise, without the prior permission of the publishers.

Red Fox Books are published by Random House Children's Publishers UK,
61–63 Uxbridge Road, London W5 5SA

www.randomhousechildrens.co.uk
www.randomhouse.co.uk

Addresses for companies within The Random House Group Limited can be found at:
www.randomhouse.co.uk/offices.htm

THE RANDOM HOUSE GROUP Limited Reg. No. 954009

A CIP catalogue record for this book is available from the British Library.

Printed in China

Penguin Random House is committed to a sustainable future for our business, our readers and
our planet. This book is made from Forest Stewardship Council® certified paper.

MIX
Paper from
responsible sources
FSC
www.fsc.org   FSC® C018179

Katie Morag
and the Two Grandmothers

Mairi Hedderwick

RED FOX

High Farm

The Holiday House

Mrs Bayview's

The Lady Arti

The Redburn
Bridge

The Village

THE ISLE of STRUAY

Grannie's

The Mainland

The Jetty

ISLE of STRUAY
SHOP & POST OFFICE

OBAN
TIMES
GET
YOUR COPY
HERE

The Shop & Post Office

One sunny Wednesday morning
Mrs McColl woke Katie Morag
early.

"Hurry up, now!" she said, drawing back the curtains. "Here comes the boat. Granma Mainland will be here soon and you've still got this room to tidy for her."

Granma Mainland lived far away in the big city. She was coming to stay with them for a holiday.

Katie Morag went with her other grandmother, Grannie Island, who lived just across the Bay, to meet the boat.

"My, you're still a smart wee Bobby Dazzler," said Neilly Beag, as he helped Granma Mainland down.

8

Grannie Island revved the engine *very* loudly. BUROOM . . . BUROOM . . . BUROOM . . .

Katie Morag watched, fascinated,
as Granma Mainland unpacked.
"Do you like this new hat I've
brought for Show Day, Katie Morag?"
Granma Mainland asked.

"Och, her and her fancy ways!"
muttered Grannie Island to herself.

Show Day was always a big event
on the Island of Struay. At the Post
Office, Mr and Mrs McColl were
rushed off their feet.

"*Look* where you're GOING!"
shouted Mrs McColl, as Katie
Morag tripped over baby Liam.

"Katie Morag, I think you'd be
better off helping Grannie Island get
Alecina ready for the Show," sighed
Mr McColl.

Alecina was Grannie Island's prize sheep. She had won the Best Ewe and Fleece Trophy for the past seven years, but she was getting old, and everyone said that Neilly Beag's April Love would win it this year.

Katie Morag ran as fast as she could, past the Show Field, where frantic last-minute preparations were in progress, and on to Grannie Island's in order to give Alecina an extra special brush and comb before the judging started.

But when Katie Morag arrived at
Grannie Island's, Alecina was up to
her horns in the Boggy Loch.

"A whole hillside to eat and she
wants *that* blade of grass!" cried
Grannie Island in a fury.

"Look at your fleece! And today
of *all* days, you old devil!" ranted
Grannie Island when they eventually
got Alecina out of the Boggy Loch.
"We'll never get these peaty stains
out in time for the Show!"

"Granma Mainland has some stuff
to make *her* hair silvery white . . ."
said Katie Morag thoughtfully.

Everyone looked in amazement
as Grannie Island's old tractor and
trailer hurtled past the Show Field,
heading for the Post Office.

"We'll be too late!" grumbled
Grannie Island.

Fortunately, no one was about
when they got home, since Mrs
McColl would certainly not have
approved of this . . .

. . . or this.

And Granma Mainland would
have been furious at this . . .

. . . not to mention this.

But all ended well. They managed to get tidied up and back to the Show Field just in time for the judging.

At the sight of Alecina's shiny
coat and curls, the judges were in
no doubt as to who should win the
Silver Trophy again this year.

That evening there was a party at Grannie Island's to celebrate.

"My, but thon old ewe is still some beauty for her age," said Neilly Beag. "Just like yourself, Granma Mainland. How do you do it?"

"Ah, that's *my* secret," said wee Granma Mainland, fluttering her eyelashes.

Katie Morag and Grannie
Island smiled at each other.
They knew some of the secret,
but would never tell.

And Grannie Island never
frowned at Granma Mainland's
"fancy ways" ever again.
I wonder why?